The Three

Retold by Alan Benjamin
Illustrated by Lilian Obligado

For Thea Feldman
—A.B.

A GOLDEN BOOK • NEW YORK
Golden Books Publishing Company, Inc., Racine, Wisconsin 53404

When Mama Pig thought her three little pigs were old enough, she packed them each a lunch, kissed them each on the cheek, and sent them out into the world to seek their fortunes.

Off they went together, each with a bright kerchief for a knapsack. When they came to a fork in the road, they bid each other good-bye and good luck. Then one went this way, one went that way, and one the other.

Soon the first little pig met a man carrying a great bundle of straw. "Please, sir," he asked, "could you spare enough straw for me to build myself a house?"

The man did as he was asked, and soon
the first little pig had built himself a cozy
little house of straw.

Before long a hungry wolf knocked at the door of the little straw house.

"Little pig, little pig, let me come in," he called.

"No, not by the hair of my chinny-chin-chin," answered the first little pig.

"Then I'll huff, and I'll puff, and I'll blow your house in," said the wolf. And, sure enough, he H-U-F-F-E-D, and he P-U-F-F-E-D, and he blew the house in.

But before the house came tumbling down, the first little pig had run out the back door and into the woods. He decided then and there to find his two brothers.

The second little pig walked along until he met a man wheeling a barrow full of sticks. "Please, sir," he asked, "could you spare enough sticks for me to build myself a house?"

The man did as he was asked, and soon
the second little pig had built himself a snug
little house of sticks.

Before long the wolf was at his door — and
he was still hungry. "Little pig, little pig, let
me come in," he called.

"No, not by the hair of my chinny-chin-
chin," answered the second little pig.

"Then I'll huff, and I'll puff, and I'll blow your house in," said the wolf. And, sure enough, he H-U-F-F-E-D, and he P-U-F-F-E-D, and he blew the house in.

But before the house came clattering down, the second little pig had climbed out the back window and run into the woods. He decided then and there to find his two brothers.

After the third little pig had walked for a while, he met a man pulling a cart heaped with bricks. "Please, sir," he asked, "could you spare enough bricks for me to build myself a house?"

The man did as he was asked, and soon
the third little pig had built himself a solid
little house of brick.

After a while, his two brothers and his
mother found their way to his new little
brick house, and they all decided to live
together once more.

One morning Mama Pig decided to make vegetable soup for lunch. She filled the big iron kettle that hung in the fireplace with water, added an apronful of fresh vegetables from the garden, and lit a fire under it.

Just as she placed the lid on the kettle, there was a knock at the door. It was the wolf, of course, and he was hungrier than ever. "Little pig, little pig, let me come in," he called.

"No, not by the hair of my chinny-chin-chin," answered the third little pig.

"Then I'll huff, and I'll puff, and I'll blow your house in," said the wolf. And, sure enough, he H-U-F-F-E-D, and he P-U-F-F-E-D, and he H-U-F-F-E-D, and he P-U-F-F-E-D, and he H-U-F-F-E-D, and he P-U-F-F-E-D, but he couldn't blow in the solid little brick house.

After the wolf had a chance to catch his breath, he knocked at the door once more. "If you won't open this door, I'll climb down your chimney, and then you'll all be sorry for the trouble you've caused me!"

Still no one opened the door, and soon the wolf could be heard climbing onto the roof of the little brick house.

Quietly the third little pig took the lid off the kettle. Then — SWOOSH — down the chimney came the wolf and — SPLASH — into the kettle he went.

Quick as a wink, the third little pig put
the lid back on the kettle — and that was the
end of the wolf.

To celebrate the occasion, Mama Pig took a crusty rutabaga pie from the cupboard. Everyone had a great big slice and washed it down with fresh cold apple cider. And that's the end of our story.